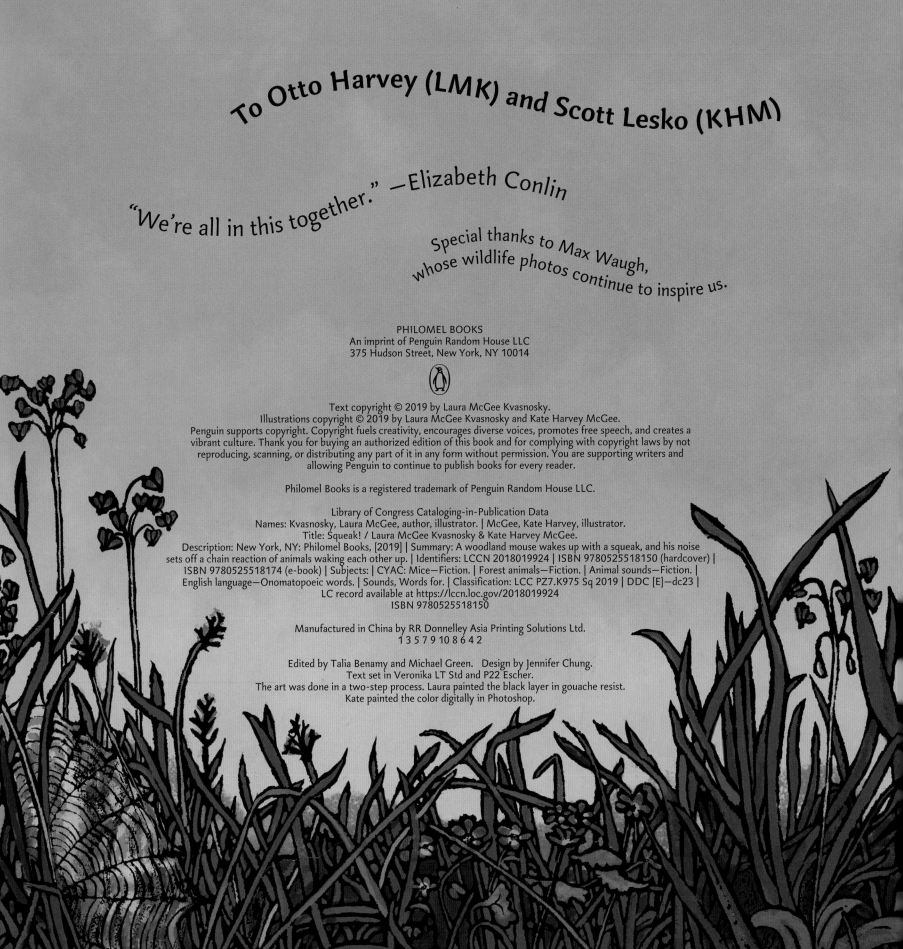

To Otto Harvey (LMK) and Scott Lesko (KHM)

"We're all in this together." —Elizabeth Conlin

Special thanks to Max Waugh, whose wildlife photos continue to inspire us.

PHILOMEL BOOKS
An imprint of Penguin Random House LLC
375 Hudson Street, New York, NY 10014

Library of Congress Cataloging-in-Publication Data
Names: Kvasnosky, Laura McGee, author, illustrator. | McGee, Kate Harvey, illustrator.
Title: Squeak! / Laura McGee Kvasnosky & Kate Harvey McGee.
Description: New York, NY: Philomel Books, [2019] | Summary: A woodland mouse wakes up with a squeak, and his noise sets off a chain reaction of animals waking each other up. | Identifiers: LCCN 2018019924 | ISBN 9780525518150 (hardcover) | ISBN 9780525518174 (e-book) | Subjects: | CYAC: Mice—Fiction. | Forest animals—Fiction. | Animal sounds—Fiction. | English language—Onomatopoeic words. | Sounds, Words for. | Classification: LCC PZ7.K975 Sq 2019 | DDC [E]—dc23 |
LC record available at https://lccn.loc.gov/2018019924
ISBN 9780525518150

Manufactured in China by RR Donnelley Asia Printing Solutions Ltd.
1 3 5 7 9 10 8 6 4 2

Edited by Talia Benamy and Michael Green.    Design by Jennifer Chung.
Text set in Veronika LT Std and P22 Escher.
The art was done in a two-step process. Laura painted the black layer in gouache resist.
Kate painted the color digitally in Photoshop.

# SQUEAK!

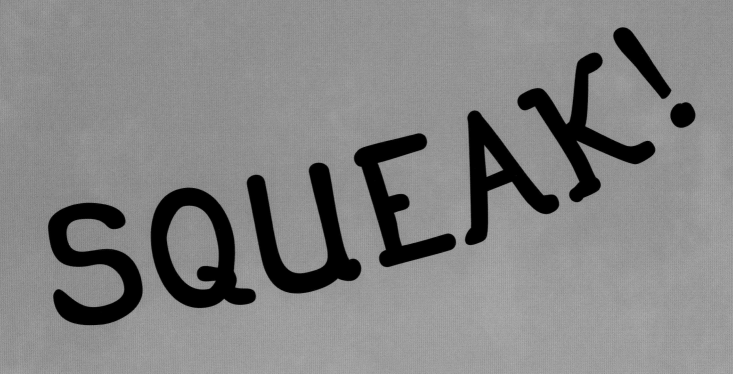

Laura McGee Kvasnosky
Kate Harvey McGee

Philomel Books

Early, early one morning, a breeze rippled
through the meadows and mountains and
tickled the ear of a small mouse.

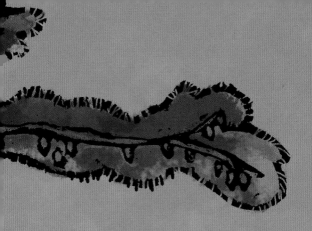

His eyes popped open.

SQUEAK!

That tiny squeak floated upward
to the chipmunks' hollow.

Out skittered the chipmunks, chittering
and chattering.
Branches shook and pinecones fell

KERPLOP!

into the river.

Trout were resting right there in the river,
dreaming their watery dreams. They leapt
awake with a splish and a splash and a

SPLISH

All that splishing and splashing woke an elk on the riverbank. He lurched up and bumped smack into a cottonwood tree.

Then WHOOOOOSH! an eagle launched
from the top of the cottonwood tree, beating
her wings against the pale morning sky.

WAH-WHOOOOSH!

WAH-WHOOOOSH!

The rush of eagle wings woke two bear cubs. Out they tumbled from their cave, their mama hot on their heels. She tried to quiet them down.

**GRRRRRRR!** she grumped.

**GR**

But already a pup over in the wolf den had heard the bears' shenanigans and started to howl.

YIP YIP YIP YIP YIP!

The pack woke up and joined in.

AAAAAOOOOOOOOOO

Their howls echoed across the cliffs and woke a bighorn lamb. When she leapt to another perch, rocks and gravel thundered to the meadow below.

BAA BAA
RUMBLE BUMBLE

The biggest bison snoozing down in the meadow startled out of his dreams. He did not like to wake up before the sun.

ARRGRUMMPH!

he bellowed, and louder,

ARRRGRUMMMPHH!

The bison's bellows billowed over the mountains and meadows and woke up everybody else. Badgers popped out of their setts. Otters and beavers splashed into the river. Raccoons rustled. Snakes hissed.

CAW CAW CAW

RUSTLE RUSTLE

SLICKERY SLICKERY

SLAPPA BAP-BAP

SWISH SWISH

RIBBIT RIBBIT

SPLASH

Frogs croaked. Bees buzzed. Foxes and jackrabbits swished through the slickery grass, while swans and loons and warblers and ravens called and twittered and cooed.

CHEE CHEE CHEE CHEE WEE WEE

WA OH OH OH OH OH

BZZZZZZZZZZZZZZZ

OONK
OONK

CHURRR

HISSSSSSSSSSSS

The small mouse heard the big ruckus and wondered, *Why is everybody up so early today?*

SQUEAK

he whispered to himself. Then he snuggled in and drifted back to sleep.